# The Wagon Train West

*Columbus, OH*

**SRAonline.com**

 **SRA**

Send all inquiries to this address:
SRA/McGraw-Hill
4400 Easton Commons
Columbus, OH  43219

ISBN: 978-0-07-608780-8
MHID: 0-07-608780-8

1 2 3 4 5 6 7 8 9  NOR  13  12  11  10  09  08  07

The McGraw-Hill Companies

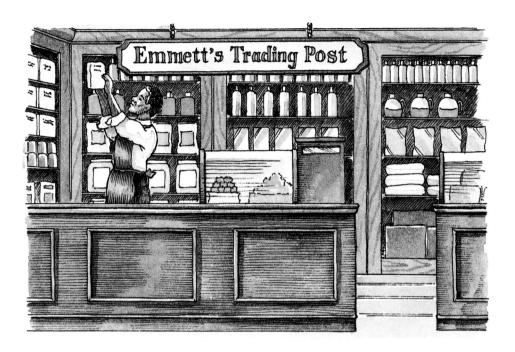

The year was 1845, and people were flocking to the West like flies to a pie at a picnic. All kinds of people—white, black, big, skinny, tall, short—were going. One thing they all had in common was Emmett's Trading Post in St. Louis. They either stopped there or started there—it didn't matter which—but they all needed provisions, and that's what Emmett had to offer.

Business at Emmett's had picked up quite a bit lately. Emmett himself had considered taking off for the West, where he had heard that the sky was bluer than the bluest blue and bigger than anything he had ever seen in his lifetime. He did not know, though, because his papa had told him over and over again to finish what he had started. And since he had started this business, he wanted to see it through.

One afternoon while Emmett was waiting on a customer, he started thinking things over, though. There was a wagon train departing in the morning—one of the last ones that would come by for a little while. He had come to St. Louis in the hopes of finding something bigger and better for himself, and he had, but he had a hankerin' for more. He knew his papa would have understood this and knew he would have been proud of Emmett's adventurous spirit. Emmett made the decision to join the wagon train.

He gave the keys to the store to his friend Jeremiah. The wagon master told him the train was pulling out at dawn. The man said, "As long as yer ready to go, you can come along, but don't be 'specting us to wait for you."

Emmett assured the wagon master that he would be ready in two shakes of a lamb's tail. The wagon master shook his head, thinking that Emmett could not possibly be ready on time.

The wagon master didn't know Emmett, though.

That night when the store closed, Emmett got to work. He hitched his oxen to his wagon and began loading it up. Like a whirlwind at work, Emmett threw supplies into the wagon faster than the winds of a twister. (That's a tornado to you cityfolk.)

When dawn came Emmett had eight hundred pounds of flour, seven hundred pounds of bacon, two hundred pounds of beans, one hundred pounds of fruit, seventy-five pounds of coffee, and twenty-five pounds of salt in his wagon. He hoped it would be enough to feed him for at least the first week of the trip. Emmett was a big man with an even bigger appetite.

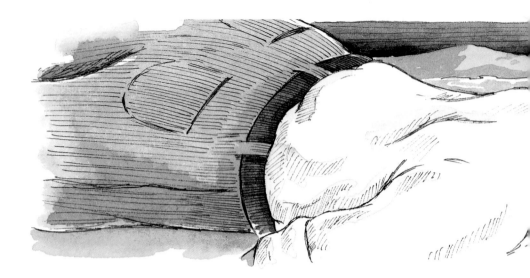

The wagon train set off across the Midwest prairie with the two dozen wagons embarking together. For the first few weeks, things moved along just fine—slow, but fine. The wagon scout left every morning and reported back to the wagon master about what was up ahead for the next day's journey. Life was sweeter than Mama's gooseberry jam.

Then the weather started changing a bit, and it rained much more than usual. That contributed to the change in pace, making it even slower. Since most everybody walked alongside their wagons, the mud made for a big mess and slowed them up even more.

One night the scout came back and said, "That there Kansas River is flooded up ahead. I'm a-feared we'll all drown!"

The wagon master thought and thought and, shaking his head, said he would sleep on it and figure it out in the morning.

Emmett overheard the wagon scout's report. He knew what he had to do, and he set about doing it. While everyone was asleep, he tiptoed out of the camp and trotted off toward the river. It was flooded, all right, but did that stop Emmett? No how, no way! He simply lay down on the ground and opened his mouth. The water from the flooded river flowed in, and Emmett swallowed and swallowed and swallowed. The river receded, and the water went down, down, down. By the time he stood up, you could not tell there had been a flood. He had even spat out the fishes that had been swirling in the rushing waters.

The next morning when the wagon train arrived at the river, they were able to make the crossing without a hitch.

Days passed and the air near the mountains grew chilly. Emmett had heard rumors that the weather on this trail could get really bad, and he shivered just thinking about it. Folks said the snowflakes on the trail were as big as quilts but not nearly as warm. Emmett supposed that that was where the expression "blanketed by snow" came from. So he was not surprised when the scout came back to the wagon train one night, talking about a terrible snowstorm ahead. He said the snow was coming down faster than a swarm of bees after honey and that he had gotten caught in it. The icicle on the end of his nose quivered as he said, "I'm a-feared we'll lose the trail!"

The wagon master thought and thought and, shaking his head, said he would sleep on it and figure it out in the morning.

Again Emmett heard the scout and the wagon master talking. Emmett knew what he had to do, and he set about doing it. While everyone was asleep, he tiptoed out of the camp and trotted off around the bend. It had snowed, all right—musta been a ragin' blizzard from what he could tell—but did that stop Emmett? No how, no way! He rubbed his arms and then his hands to warm up. He stomped his feet to get the circulation back to flowin' in his frozen toes, took a couple of deep breaths, and exhaled. He blew and he blew and he blew—matter of fact, he blew all the snow clear off the trail and then some.

The next morning when the procession got around the bend, instead of snow there was a pristine trail awaiting them. The wagon master began to think his scout might be having trouble with his eyesight.

Time passed uneventfully. The land was rough
and bumpy, and the wagon train had to move slowly.
Everyone was tired and hungry—their feet ached from
all the walking they had to do, and they were sick of
bacon and beans.

Then one evening the wagon scout returned to
camp with some devastating news. The trail they
were on would take them through a pass in the Rocky
Mountains. But the pass was obstructed with fallen
rock, dirt, and debris, built up to a point that the scout
feared they would not get through. He said, "I figure
that snowstorm set off an avalanche or somethin'. I'm
a-feared we'll never make it!"

The wagon master thought and thought and, shaking
his head, said he would sleep on it and figure it out in
the morning.

　　As Emmett was settling in for a night's sleep, he overheard the wagon master and the scout discussing the mountain pass. He was mighty exhausted, but Emmett knew what he had to do, and he set about doing it. While everyone was asleep, he tiptoed out of the camp and trotted off toward the Rocky Mountains. The debris blocking the path was high, all right, but did that stop Emmett? No how, no way! He spit in his calloused hands and rubbed them together. Then he grabbed the shovel he had brought and began to dig. He dug and he dug and he dug, and soon the mountain pass was excavated and cleared of all the fallen debris.

　　The next morning the wagon train headed for the mountain pass and found it level, clean, and altogether crossable. The wagon master shook his head at the scout.

More time passed. The expedition was more than halfway to its destination. The womenfolk talked about strawberries in California bigger than a large man's fist, and the menfolk discussed steaks that extended across the whole top of a fancy restaurant table. Children spoke of ocean waves so high you needed a ladder to climb back down.

The scout left for his ride and came back that night with terrible news. All the melting snow and rain had washed out a bridge that the wagon train had to cross to get over a huge river. He said, "I done rode up and down the bank for miles and miles. There ain't no way to cross. I'm a-feared we'll drown … again!"

The wagon master thought and thought and, shaking his head, said he would sleep on it and figure it out in the morning.

Once again Emmett overheard the conversation. He knew what he had to do, and he set about doing it. While everyone was asleep, he tiptoed out of the camp and trotted off toward the river, looking for the washed-out bridge. He found pieces of it scattered here and there, as if a giant hand had picked them up and tossed them in the air—but did that stop Emmett? No how, no way! He took a few deep breaths and pulled and pulled and pulled down trees from the nearby forest. He dove into the pile and worked so fast you would have missed it if you blinked. Before you knew it, Emmett had woven a sturdy bridge that extended from one bank of the river to the other.

The next morning the wagon train was able to make it over the river. The wagon master mumbled under his breath, "That scout …"

The bad weather seemed to be behind them. The days were getting longer, the sun was getting warmer, and the wagon train was almost there. Good thing too, because everyone was almost out of fresh drinking water.

The scout panicked one night, yelling, "How are we gonna make it through the desert with no water?"

The wagon master held a meeting and told everyone on the wagon train that the water they had left had to be rationed.

People began offering up ideas about just how to do that. Water for this, no water for that, only a little water here and there for this and that, and so on. There were too many suggestions, and only some of them made a lick of sense at all.

The wagon master thought and thought and, shaking his head, said he would sleep on it and figure it out in the morning.

The meeting disbanded, and everyone headed back to their wagons for the night. Emmett knew what he had to do, and he set about doing it. While everyone was asleep, he grabbed up a few ladles and empty water barrels and tiptoed out of the camp. He knew that the closest place for water was a lake that was a long way off, but did that stop Emmett? No how, no way! He took off, running as fast as he could, leaving a cloud of dust behind him. When he got to the lake, he scooped and scooped and scooped up water until every single barrel was full, and then he headed back to camp.

When the pioneers woke up in the morning, a barrel full of water was sitting next to each wagon.

The wagon train then crossed into the desert region, which was flat and arid. People talked about what they had longed for on the trip and what they were going to do when they got to California. The mood of the people on the wagon train was great, and spirits were elevated.

One night the wagon scout came galloping into camp, jumped off his horse, and pulled the wagon master aside. He told the wagon master that a few miles up ahead, a group of bandits had made camp right off the trail the wagons were traveling. He said, "There's mean and ornery thieves lurking out there! I'm a-feared they'll take everything we got!"

The wagon master thought and thought and, shaking his head, said he would sleep on it and figure it out in the morning.

Emmett listened to the conversation about the bandits. Emmett knew what he had to do, and he set about doing it. While everyone was asleep, he tiptoed out of camp and trotted off down the trail. Sure enough, there was a campfire, and some men were sitting around it, talking about the wagon train. The men spotted Emmett, but did that stop him? No how, no way! Emmett jumped and jumped and jumped up and down until the earth underneath him shivered and cracked and split apart, leaving the thieves on one side of the giant crevice and him and the trail on the other.

The next morning the wagon train passed the giant crevice in the ground. There was no evidence that anyone had been there. The wagon master was certain now that the scout had nothing but rocks in his head.

It was hot in the desert—unbearably hot—hotter than anyone had expected. The sun was burning down on the pioneers, making their faces look like red beets. The oxen were tired, and no one had the strength, much less desire, to talk. Children whined and complained and their mothers couldn't quiet them. There was not much farther to go on this long, long trek, but it sure felt to folks like it would take forever.

The wagon master decided to stop the day's travel and let everyone get a good night's rest. He and the wagon scout talked about the heat and the dust. The scout said, "It's so hot out here! I'm a-feared we'll bake like pies in an oven!"

The wagon master thought and thought and, shaking his head, said he would sleep on it and figure it out in the morning.

Emmett was too hot to sleep, and he overheard the wagon master and the scout talking. He knew what he had to do, and he set about doing it. While everyone was asleep, he tiptoed out of camp and trotted on down the trail, keeping his eyes peeled for a way to relieve the miserable heat.

He spotted some prickly-pear cactus and got a brilliant idea. There were thorns all over them, but did that stop Emmett? No how, no way! He gathered hundreds of cactus plants in his hands and stuck them all together to make one giant fan. As he moved the fan up and down, it generated a breeze. The gentle breeze wafted through the desert all the way to the wagon train, cooling everything and everyone.

Since everyone on the wagon train had cooled off and gotten a good night's sleep, they were ready to tackle the rest of the desert and the last leg of the journey. It helped that they had only about fifty miles to go.

20

The wagon scout reported back every night that it was smooth sailing from there on out. (Admittedly this made the wagon master nervous, since the scout had been wrong every other time.)

Then something happened that the scout could not have foreseen. When the train was about twenty miles from their destination, a rickety wheel on the wagon master's wagon broke, splintering into a million pieces. The wagon train came to a halt. No one could believe it. After all this time and with only a little bit left to go, they were held up by a broken wheel.

Everyone argued about what to do. One group thought they should stay and try to repair the wheel. The other thought they should divide the wagon master's things among them and abandon his wagon. What would they do with the oxen, though? Who would take what?

Emmett knew what he had to do, and he set about doing it. He trotted over to the broken-down wagon and curled himself around the axle. He knew they had twenty miles to go, but did that stop him? No how, no way! With a yell to the oxen to giddyup, the wagon lurched forward on three wheels and Emmett. The wagon train was back in business, and before you knew it, the train had crossed over the border and into California. They had done it—they had made the trip from St. Louis to California and lived to tell the tale!

So what ever happened to those pioneers? Well, they finally realized that it had been Emmett who had helped them out all along on the long journey. It was that last bit when he had made himself into a wheel that had done it.

"Why did you help us, Emmett?" they asked while thanking him.

Emmett told them that his African name was Emeka, which meant "Great Deeds." He said, "I have been able to do great deeds for as long as I can remember, and my papa always told me to use my strengths to help people. So I did and I do." Emmett grinned.

Later, when the people from the wagon train settled in California, they built a statue of Emmett for their town with a plaque that read, "Thanks to Emeka."

And what about Emmett? Well, he thought one wagon train trip was enough for anyone's lifetime. He opened up a general store, much like the one he had had in St. Louis. The wagon master retired and helped Emmett in the store part-time. He was not about to go on another wagon train trip without Emmett, even if the wagon master finally knew his scout wasn't crazy.

The wagon scout opened a sightseeing business in another city. He came back to the pioneers' town once a year to see his old friends. They traded stories about their adventures on the wagon train. Each time someone told a story, Emmett's great deeds grew even greater, but no one ever told anyone outside their group about the trip. You kinda had to be on that trip to believe it, so there wasn't much point in telling anyone else.

Until now.

# Vocabulary

**prairie** (prâ´ rē) (page 6) *n*. A large area of level or rolling land with grass and few or no trees.

**procession** (prə sesh´ ən) (page 9) *n*. A group of persons moving forward in a line or in a certain order.

**rationed** (rash´ ənd) (page 14) *v*. Past tense of **ration:** To limit to fixed portions.

**ladles** (lā´ dəlz) (page 15) *n*. Plural of **ladle:** A spoon with a long handle and a bowl shaped like a cup. It is used to scoop up liquids.

**region** (rē´ jən) (page 16) *n*. Any large area or territory.

**longed** (longd) (page 16) *v*. Past tense of **long:** To want very much; yearn.

**lurking** (lûr´ king) (page 16) *v*. A form of the verb **lurk:** To lie hidden and quiet, preparing to attack.

**evidence** (e´ və dəns) (page 17) *n*. Proof of something.

**rickety** (ri´ ki tē) (page 21) *adj*. Likely to fall or break; shaky.

# Comprehension Focus: Predicting

1. Reread page twelve. What did you predict Emmett might do next?

2. What do you predict Emmett might do in the future? Why do you think so?